SNOOPY'S
Book of Opposites

Peanuts® characters created and drawn by Charles M. Schulz

Text by Nancy Hall

Background illustrations by Art and Kim Ellis

A GOLDEN BOOK • NEW YORK
Western Publishing Company, Inc., Racine, Wisconsin 53404

work

play

night

day

happy

sad

good times

and bad

up

down

round and round

cold

hot

one friend

a lot

dirty   clean

in between

awake   asleep

shallow   deep

in

out

be quiet

shout

big

small

short

tall

slow

fast

laugh

cry

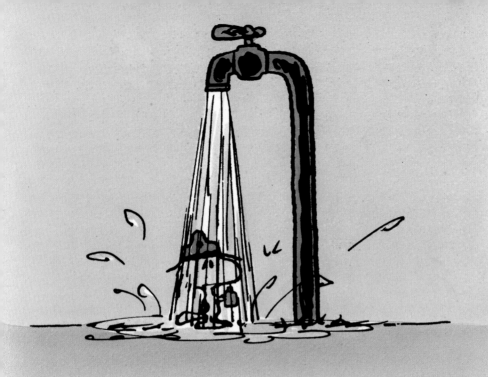

wet

dry

stand

sit